ALFIE
and the
Birthday
Surprise

Other books about Alfie:

Alfie Gets in First
Alfie's Feet
Alfie Gives a Hand
An Evening at Alfie's
Alfie Wins a Prize
Alfie Weather

Annie Rose is my Little Sister
The Big Alfie and Annie Rose Storybook
The Big Alfie Out of Doors Storybook
Rhymes for Annie Rose
Alfie's Alphabet
Alfie's Numbers

ALFIE AND THE BIRTHDAY SURPRISE
A RED FOX BOOK 978 1 86230 837 4
First published in Great Britain by The Bodley Head,
an imprint of Random House Children's Books
The Bodley Head edition published 1997
Red Fox edition published 2004
This edition published 2008 for Index Books Ltd
Copyright © Shirley Hughes, 1982
The right of Shirley Hughes to be identified as the author and illustrator of this work
has been asserted in accordance with the Copyright, Designs and Patents Act 1988.
All rights reserved.
Red Fox Books are published by Random House Children's Books,
61-63 Uxbridge Road, London W5 5SA,
a division of The Random House Group Ltd,
Addresses for companies within The Random House Group Limited
can be found at: www.randomhouse.co.uk/offices.htm
THE RANDOM HOUSE GROUP Limited Reg. No. 954009
www.rbooks.co.uk
A CIP catalogue record for this book is available from the British Library.
Printed in China

ALFIE
and the Birthday Surprise

Shirley Hughes

RED FOX

Alfie lived in the city with his mum and dad and his little
sister, Annie Rose. Right across the street lived their good
friends the MacNallys. There were Bob and Jean MacNally,
their daughter Maureen and their old cat Smoky.

Every morning, when Maureen set off to school and Bob
MacNally went to catch his bus to work, they waved to Alfie
and Annie Rose and Alfie and Annie Rose waved back.

Smoky was always there to see them off. And on fine
evenings he would sit on the wall for a long time waiting
for them to come back. Alfie's cat Chessie and Smoky were
not good friends. They eyed each other suspiciously from
opposite sides of the street. But Bob MacNally told Alfie
that Smoky was getting too old to pick fights.

The MacNallys were all very fond of Smoky. But Bob and he were special friends. When Bob came home from work he always stopped for a chat with Smoky.

Once, when Smoky was frightened up a tree and got stuck, Bob spent a whole afternoon trying to coax him down. 'It's his back legs, you see,' Bob told Alfie. 'I'm afraid he's not as young as he used to be.'

Smoky spent most of his day asleep in his favourite place by the kitchen radiator, or dozing in a patch of sunlight.

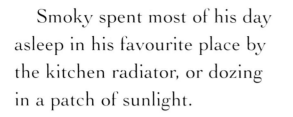

But in the evenings he would jump on to Bob MacNally's lap and they would watch television together.

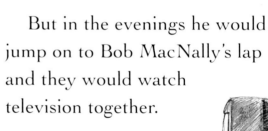

Smoky never wanted to play. When Alfie was visiting the MacNallys he would try pulling a piece of string across the floor and twitching the end, hoping that Smoky would chase after it. But Smoky only opened one slit of an eye, cocked his ears half-heartedly and went back to sleep.

If Alfie picked him up he made bad-tempered noises which meant he wanted to be left alone.

Smoky just wanted to sleep... and sleep...

One morning, Maureen came over to Alfie's house before breakfast. She was very sad. She told them that Smoky had died in the night.

'He was nearly as old as I am,' Maureen told them tearfully. 'And that's pretty old for a cat!'

Alfie was sad about Smoky being dead. 'We won't see him again, will we?' he said to Mum. 'Why did Smoky have to be dead?' he wanted to know.

'Well, he was very old and tired and he had come to the end of his life,' said Mum. 'But it was a happy life, and we'll all remember him fondly!'

Smoky was buried under a bush in the MacNallys' back garden. Maureen made a memorial for him in her woodwork class at school. Alfie helped her put it up.

She had written on it in beautiful writing:

In memory of
SMOKY
A good friend

They all cried over it, and then they began to feel better.
All except Bob.

Smoky had been his special friend and he missed him a
lot, especially in the evenings when he came home from
work and there was no Smoky waiting on the garden wall.

'It's Dad's birthday next week,' Maureen told Mum and Alfie when she was sitting in their kitchen at tea-time. 'He'll be fifty-two. And he says he doesn't want any presents at all. Not even any cards.'

'Not even balloons?' asked Alfie.

'No, nothing. He really is fed up,' said Maureen gloomily. 'And Mum says she doesn't know what to do to cheer him up.'

'He's missing Smoky, I expect,' said Mum.

Then Alfie said, 'Let's make a party for him!'

Everyone thought that was a wonderful idea. But they decided to keep it a secret until the day came. A surprise birthday party for Bob MacNally!

'When we go shopping you can choose a present for him,'
Mum told Alfie.

They looked at a great many things until they decided
on a smart pair of red socks, Alfie's favourite colour.
Mum bought a box of mint chocolates and some pretty
wrapping paper.

The party was such a big secret that Jean MacNally came over to Alfie's house specially to make the birthday cake in their kitchen. Alfie helped her to put on the candles – five blue ones and two pink ones.

The day before the surprise party all Bob's presents were ready. Jean had knitted him a sweater.

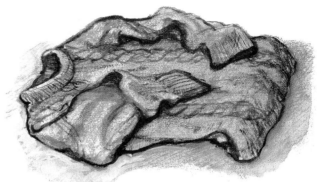

Mum and Dad had bought him a pot plant and Annie Rose was giving him a jug with a picture of the sun, moon and stars on it.

'What's your present?' Alfie asked Maureen. But she just looked mysterious and said she wasn't telling, not yet.
'I'll let you know this evening,' she promised.

Annie Rose was already asleep and Alfie was in his
dressing gown having a story when Maureen rang the
doorbell. She was carrying a basket tied up with string.
'Is that the present?' asked Alfie, very excited.
'Yes. You can see inside if you like,' said Maureen.

She put the basket down carefully in the middle of the floor and undid the string. Then she lifted the lid just a tiny bit. Alfie looked inside.

It was something alive! He saw two very bright eyes and a pink nose with white whiskers.

Then a soft paw shot out and patted his finger.

'Oh Maureen, it's a kitten,' said Mum.

'I got him from a friend at school,' said Maureen, beaming. 'Will you look after him till tomorrow? It's got to be a real surprise.'

'Oh YES!' shouted Alfie.

Mum said that they could, as it was just for the one night. 'But we'll have to be careful that Chessie doesn't meet him or she might be jealous,' she told Alfie.

'The kitten can sleep in my room,' said Alfie.

That night, Alfie and the kitten settled down together. Or tried to settle down. It wasn't very easy because the kitten kept patting the edge of Alfie's quilt and trying to climb up it. Then he got on to the bed and started a game of hide and seek.

At last he curled up and went to sleep. Alfie loved feeling him at the end of his bed. But he would not have wanted him there every night.

The next day, after Bob had gone to work, they were very busy going to and fro across the street and getting the party ready. Alfie and Maureen fed the kitten and put him in his basket. They hid him in the little room where the MacNallys kept their washing machine. At first the kitten did not like being in there.

'Don't worry – it won't be for long,' whispered Alfie. Soon the kitten stopped scratching and was quiet.

At six o'clock everything was ready. They put out
the lights and waited in the dark. At last they heard
Bob coming up the front steps.

They all kept as quiet as mice – even Annie Rose!
Alfie was so excited he had to cling on to Dad's hand
as Bob opened the front door.

'Hello? I'm home!' he called. Silence. Then he walked into the sitting room. On went the lights and they all burst out singing 'Happy Birthday to You!' At first Bob was so surprised he just stood there with his eyes and mouth wide open. Then he began to smile.

He was very pleased with his
birthday tea and his presents.

He opened them all one by one.

Best of all was when Maureen, helped by Alfie,
brought in the basket. Bob untied the string and
out jumped the kitten! Right away he started a
game with Bob's shoelaces.

Bob MacNally called the kitten Boots.

Boots was wonderfully good at inventing games. When Alfie pulled a piece of screwed-up paper across the floor, Boots lay in wait for it and then pounced.

He tossed it in the air and bicycled on it furiously with his little back legs.

Alfie showed Annie Rose how to play with Boots
and how not to squeeze him too hard.

Boots soon settled down as one of the MacNally family and Bob grew very fond of him. Though, of course, they never forgot dear old Smoky.

Alfie and Boots became great friends. Alfie was quite sure that Boots remembered how once, before the MacNallys' surprise birthday party, he had slept a whole night on the end of Alfie's bed.